THE WEDDING OF MISTRESS FOX

Text copyright © 1994 by Philip H. Bailey
Illustrations copyright © 1994 by Gavin Bishop

Published in the United States by North-South Books Inc., New York.
Published simultaneously in Great Britain, Canada, Australia, and
New Zealand in 1994 by North-South Books, an imprint of
Nord-Süd Verlag AG, Gossau Zürich, Switzerland.

Library of Congress Cataloging-in-Publication Data
Bailey, Philip H.
The wedding of Mistress Fox / by Jacob & Wilhelm Grimm ; retold
by Philip H. Bailey ; illustrated by Gavin Bishop.
Summary: As she rejects suitor after suitor, the recently widowed Mistress Fox
almost dispairs of finding a new husband with the same wonderful qualities as the late Mr. Fox.
ISBN 1-55858-335-1 (TRADE BINDING)   ISBN 1-55858-336-X (LIBRARY BINDING)
[1. Fairy tales. 2. Folklore—Germany. 3. Foxes—Folklore. 4. Animals—Folklore.]
I. Grimm, Jacob, 1785-1863. II. Grimm, Wilhelm, 1786-1859.
III. Bishop, Gavin, 1946-   ill. IV. Wedding of Mrs. Fox V. Title.
PZ8.B158we   1994   398.2'452—dc20
[E]   94-9387

A CIP catalogue record for this book is available from The British Library

The artwork was prepared with pen-and-ink and watercolor
Typography by Marc Cheshire
1 3 5 7 9 TB 10 8 6 4 2
1 3 5 7 9 LB 10 8 6 4 2
Printed in Belgium

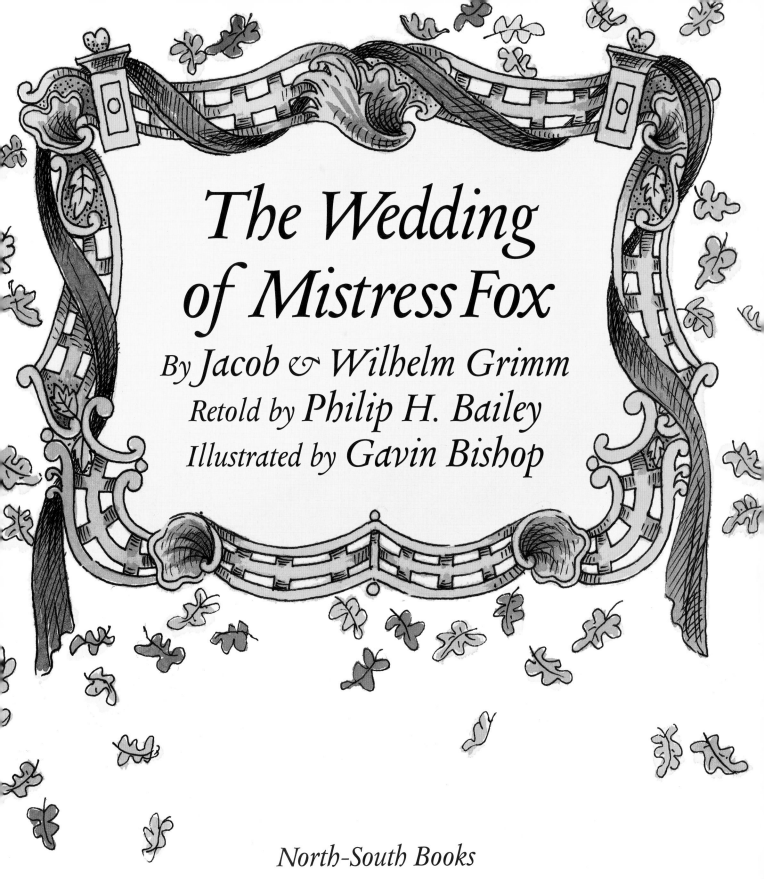

The Wedding
of Mistress Fox

By *Jacob* & *Wilhelm Grimm*
Retold by *Philip H. Bailey*
Illustrated by *Gavin Bishop*

North-South Books

New York ❧ *London*

When old Mr. Fox died, good Mistress Fox, his wife, went straight to her room, opened her closet, and took out her very best dress. It was a black dress. She put it on and sat there in state.

"I'm in retirement," she told the maid. No one could have looked more dignified.

The maid remained below, prepared the meals, and gossiped with the villagers. The maid was not unhappy: she had never liked Old Mr. Fox.

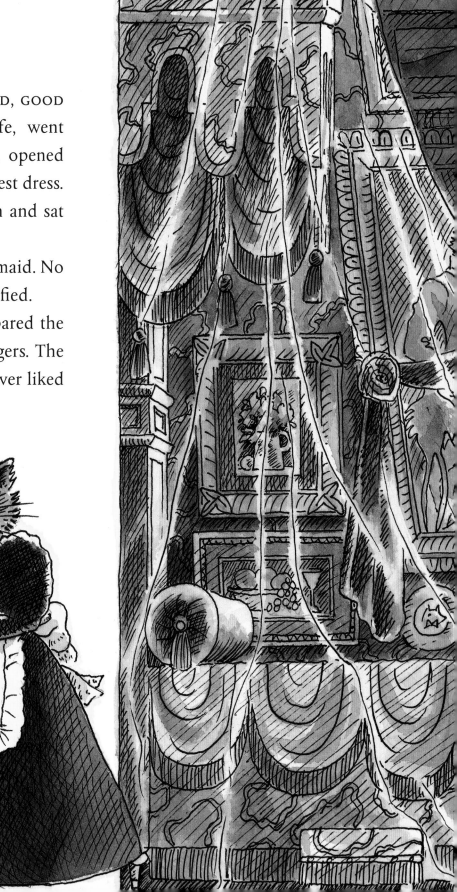

Mistress Fox was regarded in the village as a "great beauty." Master Wolf
was not the *only* gentleman to think of presenting himself as a suitable
mate—but he was the *first* to do so.

The cat was in the kitchen when she heard a *knock! knock! knock!* at the front door.

She opened it and there stood the wolf. He bowed gravely and said,
"Good day, Miss Kitty, so pert and pretty.
What is it that you cook today?"
The cat answered,
"Bread I bake and cake so fine.
Would it please you, sir, to dine?"

"Thank you, no," said the wolf. "That is most kind, but I come to inquire for your mistress. How does she and is she at home?"

The cat replied,

"All dressed in black, her room she keeps,

Her eyes are red, she sighs, she weeps.

Her sorrow gives her no relief:

Old Foxy's dead, and that's her grief."

The wolf listened politely and said,
"Her sadness may be thus, 'tis true,
But all things pass and this will too.
Go tell her that I've come to woo
And offer her a heart that's new."

Up the stairs goes the cat—*trip, trip, trip*.
On the bedroom door, she raps—*tap, tap, tap*.

"Good Mistress Fox, are you within?"

"Yes, yes, my little cat, I am."

"A suitor's come; what shall I say?
Must he go or may he stay?"

"First tell me what he's like," said good
Mistress Fox. "Does the gentleman, perchance, wear red trousers?"

"No, he does not," answered the cat. "The
trousers are gray."

"Then I won't see him," replied the lady
firmly.

So the cat ran back down stairs and sent
the unhappy wolf away.

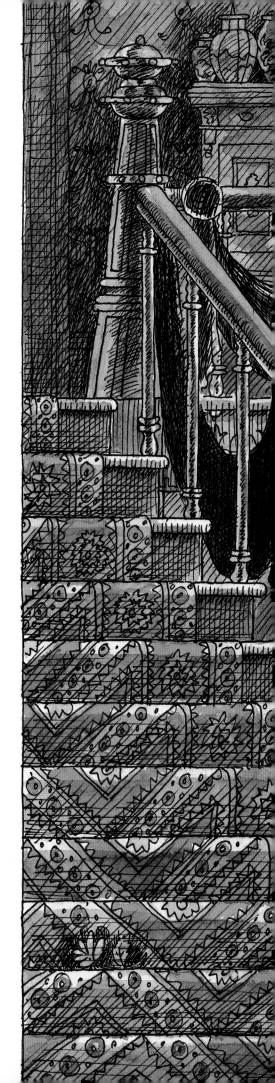

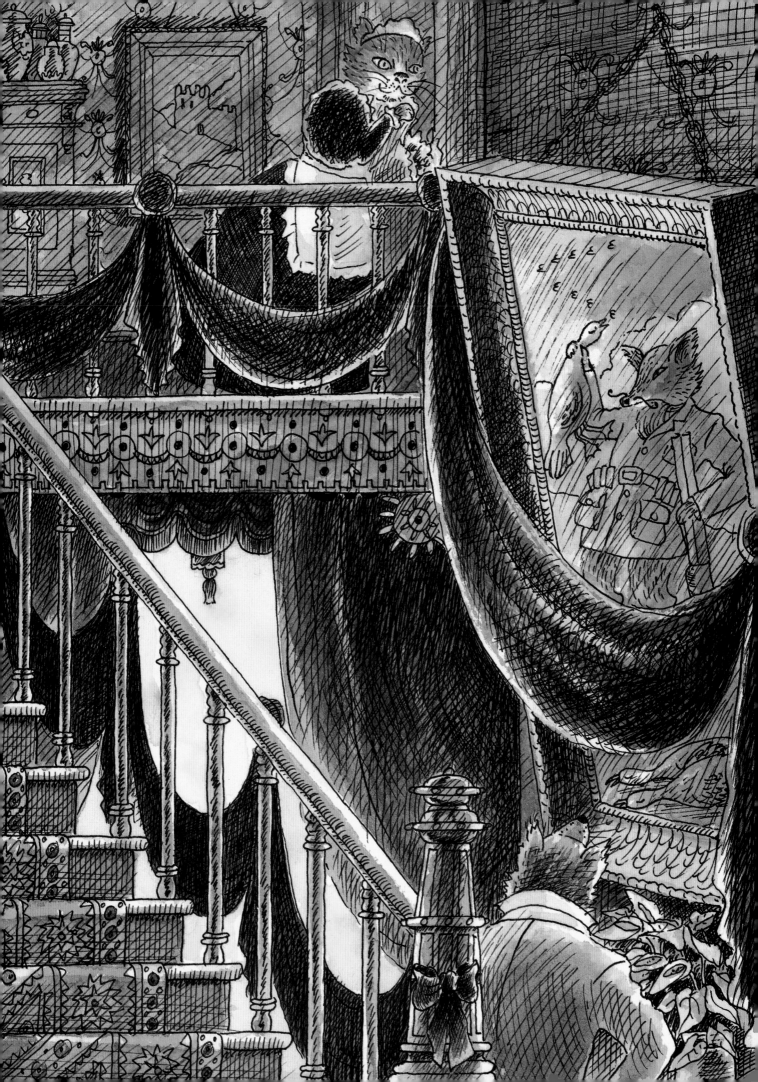

Soon there was another knock upon the door. It was another suitor.

Again the cat mounts the stairs—*trip, trip, trip*—and on the bed-room door gives a gentle rap—*tap, tap, tap*.

"Good Mistress Fox, are you within?"

"Yes, yes, my little cat, I am."

"A suitor's come; what shall I say?
Must he go or may he stay?"
"Does the gentleman, perchance, have a sharp nose?"
"No, he does not."
"Then I won't see him."

So the dog was likewise sent away.

One by one came other hopeful suitors.

None, however, possessed the features required.
Of each, the lady said, most firmly, "I won't see him; he won't do."

At length came young Master Fox. He was exceedingly polite.

Once again, the cat mounts the stairs—*trip, trip, trip.*

Once again she gives a gentle rap—*tap, tap, tap.*

"A suitor's come; what shall I say?

Must he go or may he stay?"

"First tell me what he's like. Does he, perchance, wear red trousers?"
"Oh, yes—and a red jacket, too!"

"Does he, perchance, have a tail tipped in white?"
"Oh, yes—a very bushy one, too."

"Does he, perchance, have short ears?"
"Oh, yes—short and pointed."

"Does he, perchance, have a nose that's sharp?"

"Yes, yes—sharp and inky black."

"And a mouth that's slim and narrow?"

"As slim and narrow as one could wish."

On hearing this report, good Mistress Fox rose from her chair and cried, "Then I'll see him!"

The meeting was most agreeable.

Then the widow retired to change her clothes, and as she did,
she sang,

"Clean the house and make it shine.
Get rid of that old spouse of mine!
Home he carried many a hen
And luscious goose; ah, but then
He kept them for his own delight
And never offered me a bite!
Oh, he was selfish, cold, unbending;
But now I see a happy ending."

The wedding that followed soon after was a very grand affair.
Everyone came—even the disappointed suitors—and they ate and ate
and danced and danced until dawn.

Young Master Fox proved a most loving husband.
And the cat? Well, she gets fatter every day!